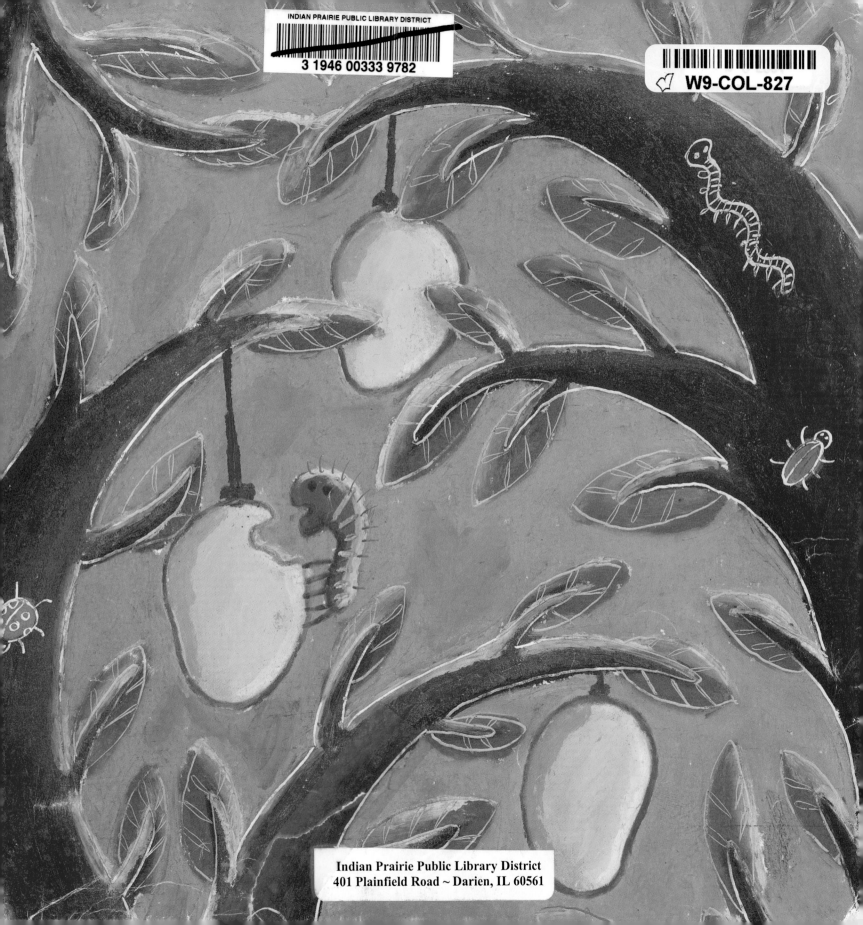

For Amy

Clarion Books
a Houghton Mifflin Company imprint
215 Park Avenue South, New York, NY 10003

Copyright © 2003 by An Vrombaut
First published as *Smile, Crocodile, Smile* in Great Britain in 2003 by
Oxford University Press. Published in the United States in 2003.

The text was set in Kristen Normal.
The illustrations were executed in pastel.

Printed in Singapore by Imago

ISBN: 0-618-33379-7
LC#: 2002151445

Full cataloging information is available from the Library of Congress.

10 9 8 7 6 5 4 3 2 1

Clarabella's Teeth

An Vrombaut

Clarion Books • New York

It's time to wake up.

Ruby brushes her rabbit teeth.

Liam brushes his leopard teeth.

Max brushes his monkey teeth.

Zoë brushes her zebra teeth.

And Clarabella?

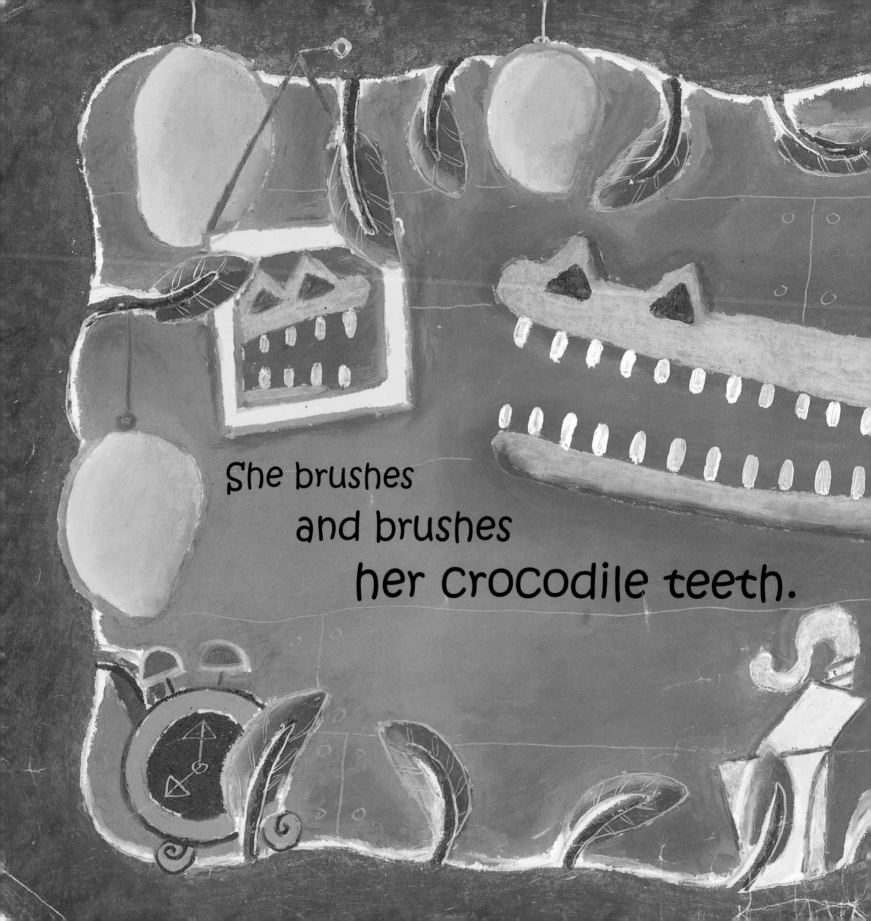

She brushes
and brushes
her crocodile teeth.

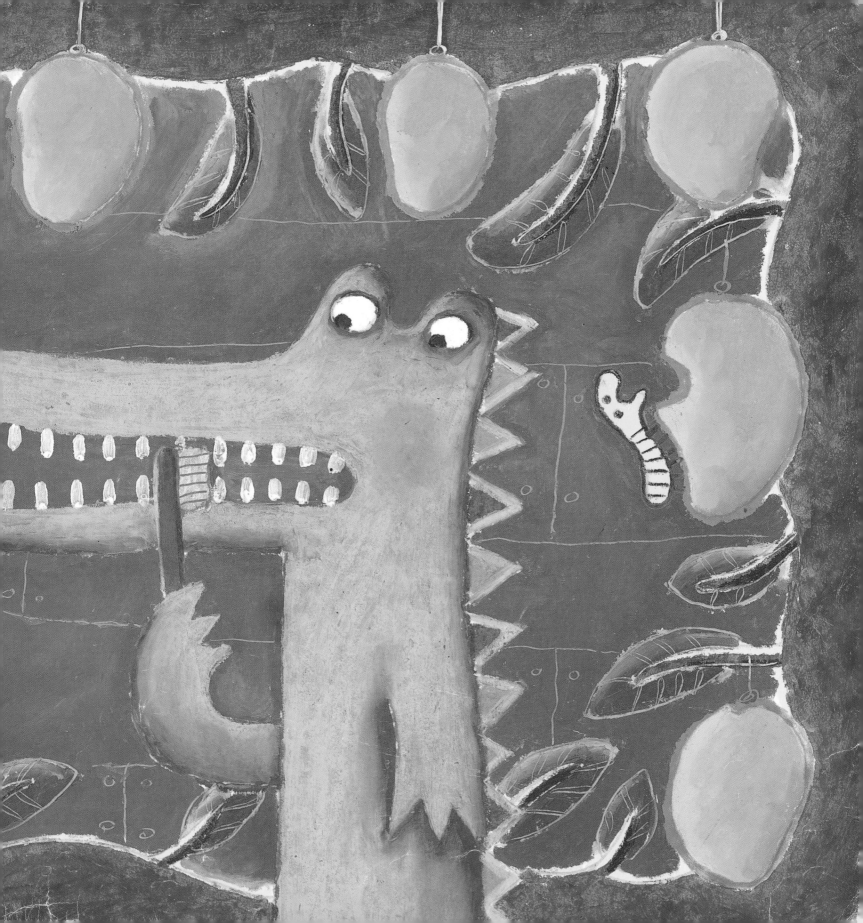

It's playtime.

Ruby builds a sandcastle.

Liam races on his scooter.

Max
makes
a mess.

Zoë plays with a puzzle.

And Clarabella?

She brushes
and brushes
and brushes
her crocodile teeth.

It's lunchtime.

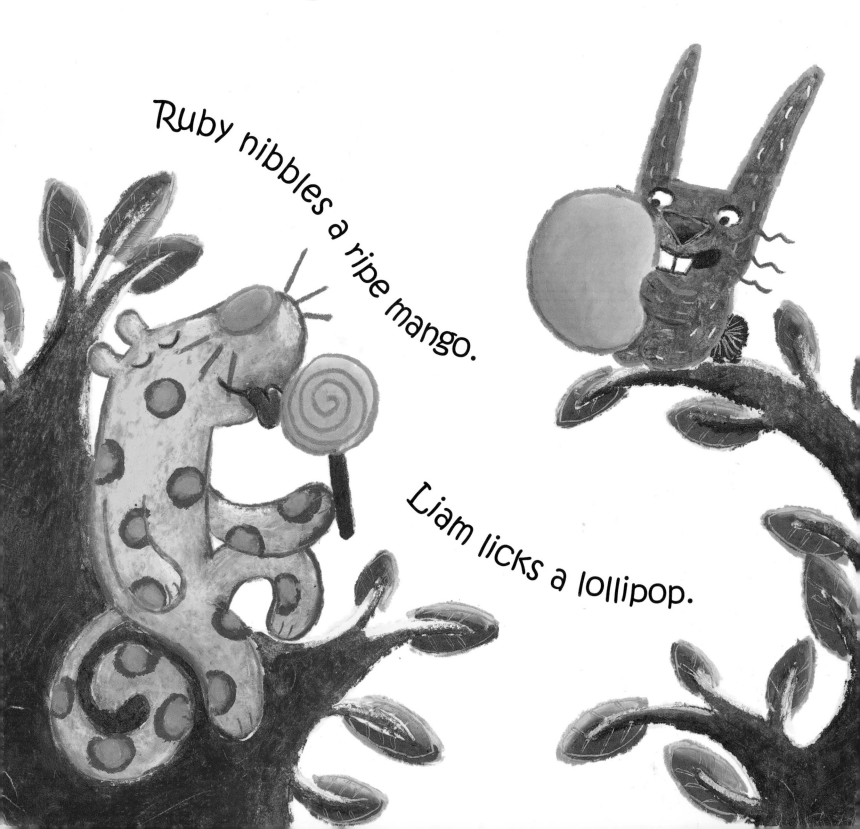

Ruby nibbles a ripe mango.

Liam licks a lollipop.

Max sips a milkshake.

Zoë munches
a sandwich.

And Clarabella?

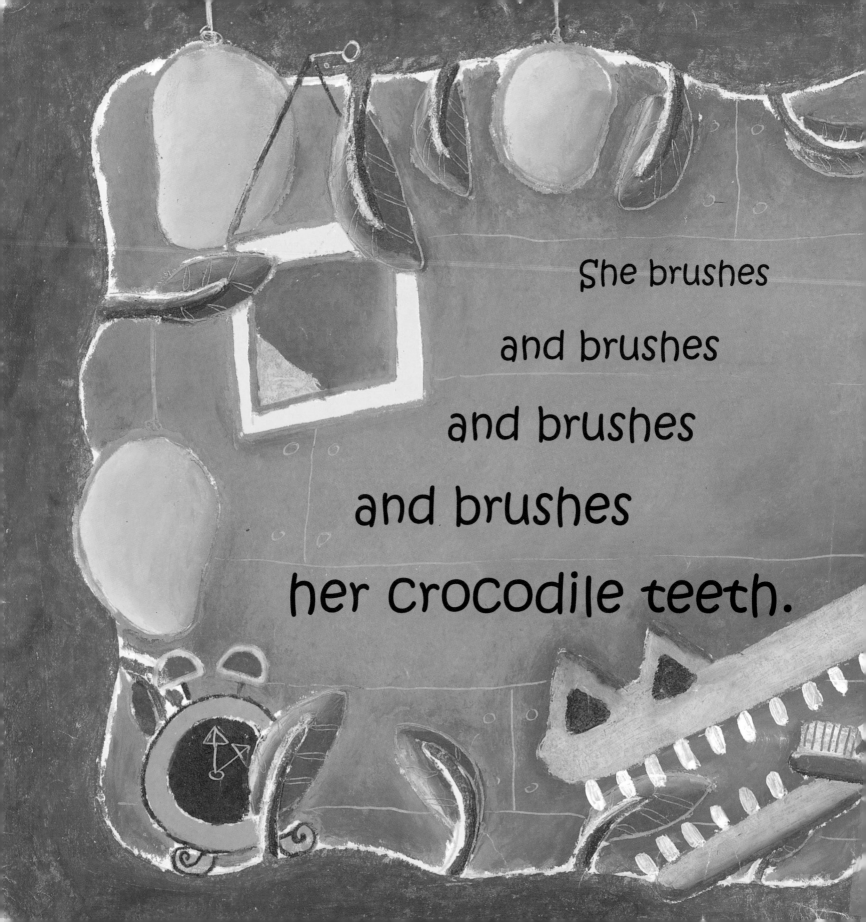

She brushes
and brushes
and brushes
and brushes
her crocodile teeth.

It's tumble time.

Ruby rolls over.

Liam leaps.

Max bounces up and down.

Zoë spins round and round and round and round.

And Clarabella?

She has brushed ALL
her crocodile teeth
and is ready
to play!

But where are her friends?

They're getting ready for bed.

"It's time to brush
our teeth," say Zoë
and Liam
and Max
and Ruby.

And Clarabella?

She sighs a
L O N G
crocodile
sigh . . .

Then Ruby has an idea.

It's a surprise!

A crocodile toothbrush for Clarabella!

"Hurray!" cheer Ruby and Liam
and Max and Zoë.
"Tomorrow we can all play
together."

And Clarabella?

She smiles a **BIG** crocodile smile!